SPACEBOT

SPACEBOT

Mike Twohy

A PAULA WISEMAN BOOK · SIMON & SCHUSTER BOOKS FOR YOUNG READERS
New York London Toronto Sydney New Delhi

SIMON & SCHUSTER BOOKS FOR YOUNG READERS

An imprint of Simon & Schuster Children's Publishing Division

1230 Avenue of the Americas, New York, New York 10020

For information about special discounts for bulk purchases, please contact

Simon & Schuster Special Sales at 1-866-506-1949 or business@simonandschuster.com.

The Simon & Schuster Speakers Bureau can bring authors to your live event.

For more information or to book an event,

contact the Simon & Schuster Speakers Bureau at 1-866-248-3049

or visit our website at www.simonspeakers.com.

Book design by Alicia Mikles

The text for this book was set in Chaloops Decaf.

The illustrations for this book were rendered in watercolor and felt pen.

Manufactured in China

0320 SCP

First Edition

2 4 6 8 10 9 7 5 3 1

Library of Congress Cataloging-in-Publication Data

Names: Twohy, Mike, author, illustrator.

Title: Spacebot / Mike Twohy.

Description: First edition. | New York : Simon & Schuster Books for Young Readers, [2020]

"A Paula Wiseman Book." | Audience: Ages 4–8. | Audience: Grades 2–3.

Summary: When a mysterious visitor arrives from outer space one night, a family dog makes an unexpected friend.

Identifiers: LCCN 2019028340 (print) | LCCN 2019028341 (eBook) | ISBN 9781534444362 (hardback) | ISBN 9781534444379 (eBook)

Subjects: CYAC: Stories in rhyme. | Extraterrestrial beings—Fiction. | Robots—Fiction. | Dogs—Fiction.

Classification: LCC PZ8.3.T85194 Sp 2020 (print) | LCC PZ8.3.T85194 (ebook) | DDC [E]—dc23

LC record available at https://lccn.loc.gov/2019028340

For Linda
and Hobs

Late at night
distant light!

"We can't sleep!"

Something's strange.
Feel a change.

Getting bright.

Scary sight.

Shakes with fear.

Almost here!

Comes down hard.
Shakes the yard.

Opens wide.

Peeks outside.

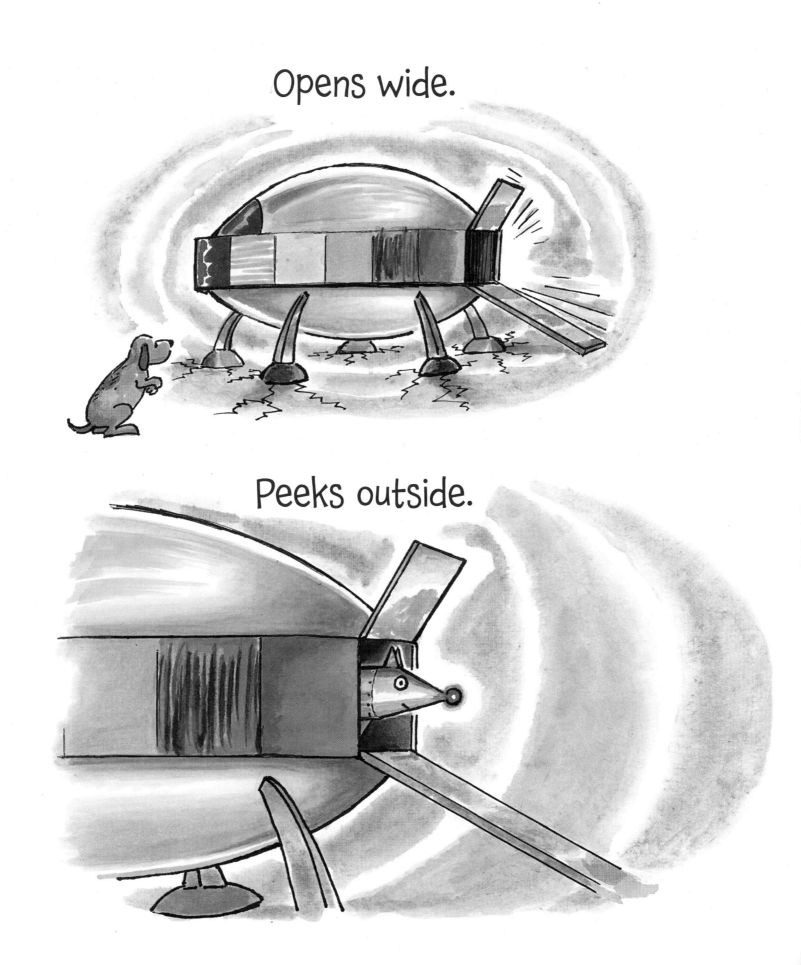

"WOW!
Yippee!"

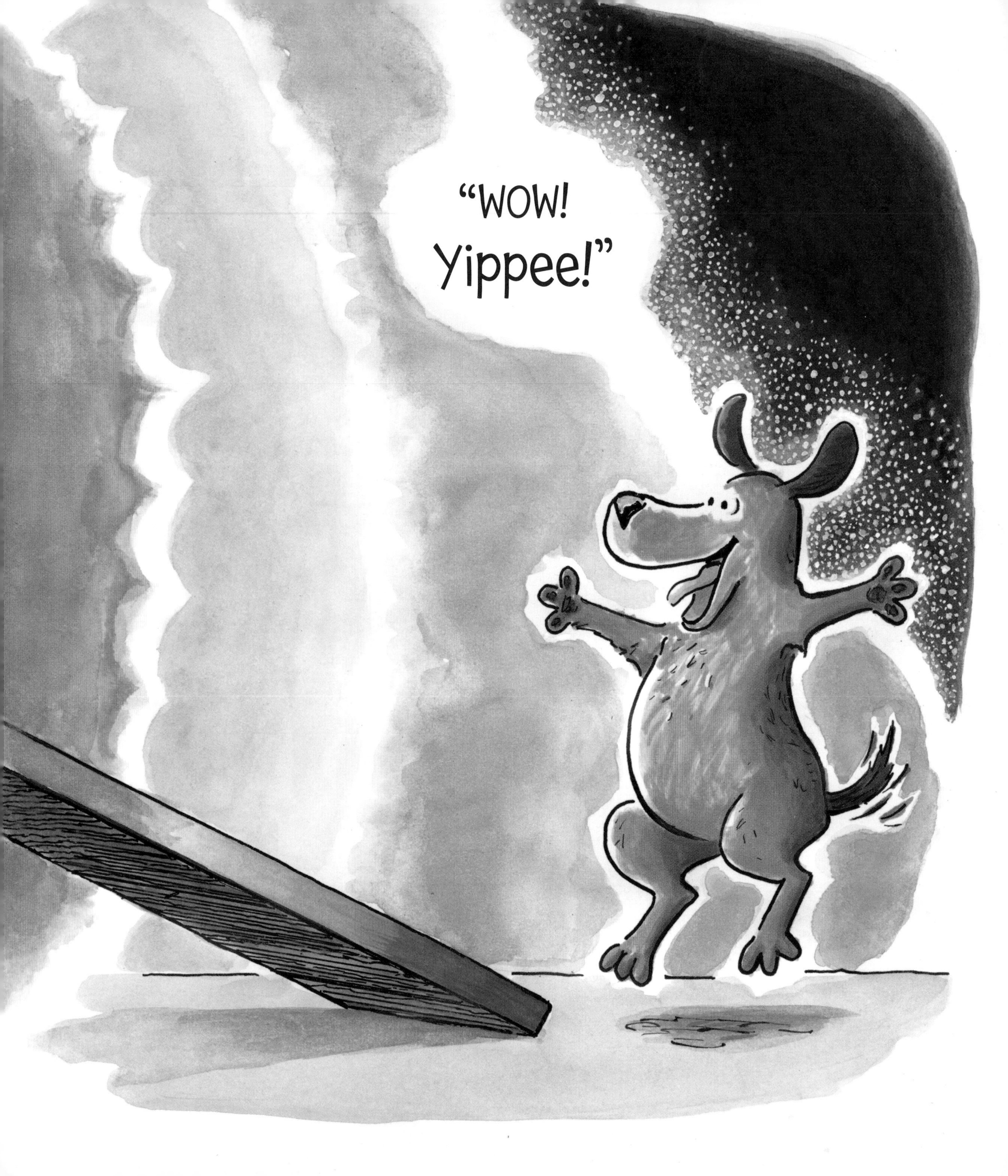

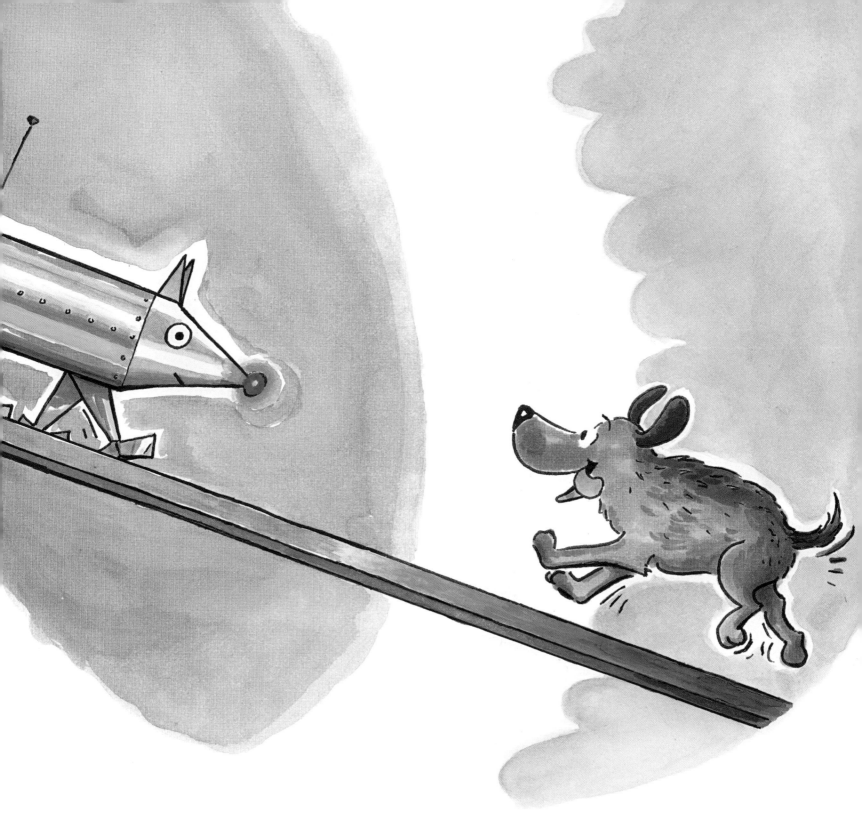

"You're like me!"

Walks away.

"Bow-wow-wow?"

"Beep-beep-pow."

Hears a cheer.

"Spacebot's here!!!"

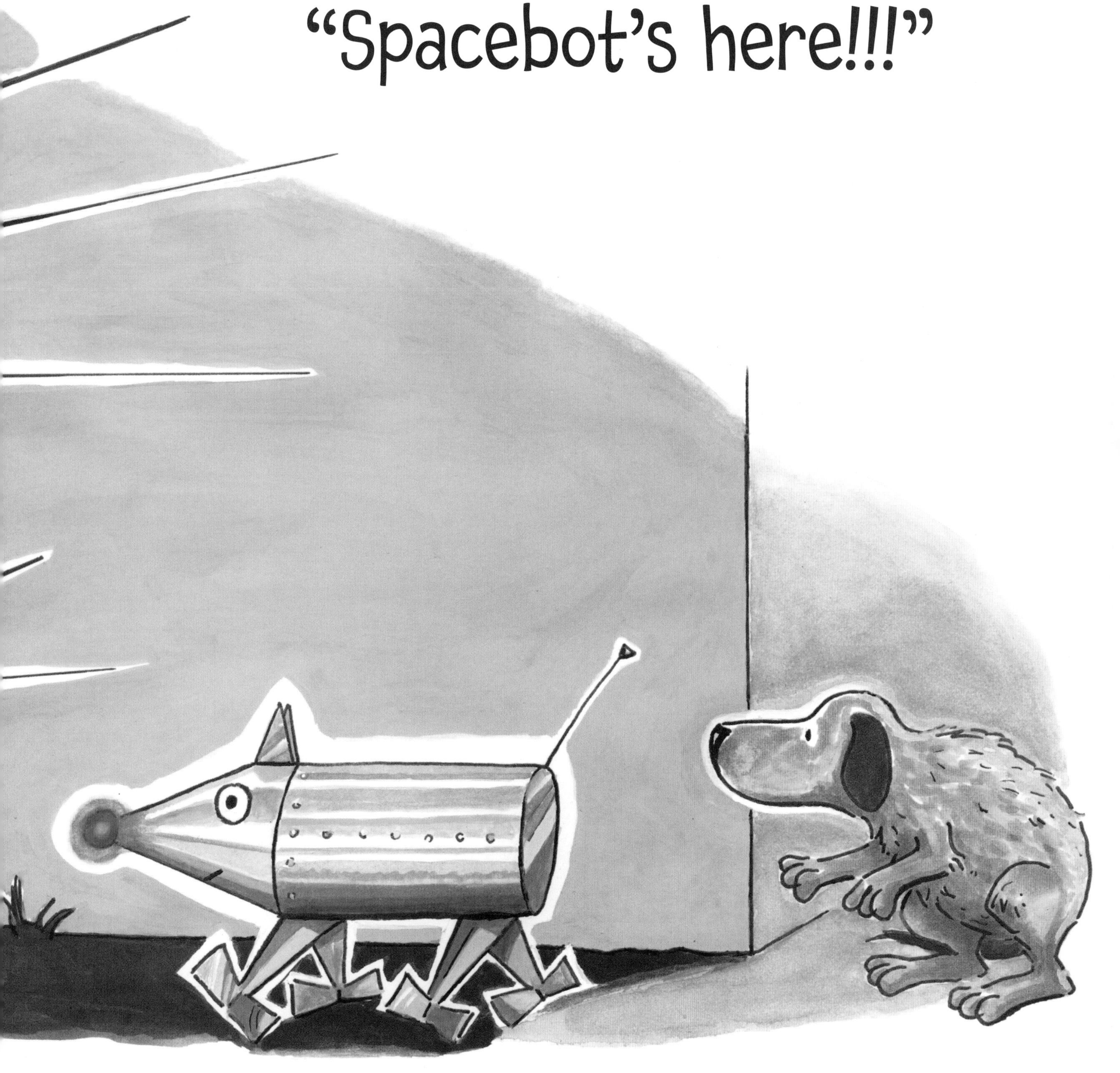

"You're like us!"

What a fuss.

Pup's left out.
Starts to pout.

Points to sky.

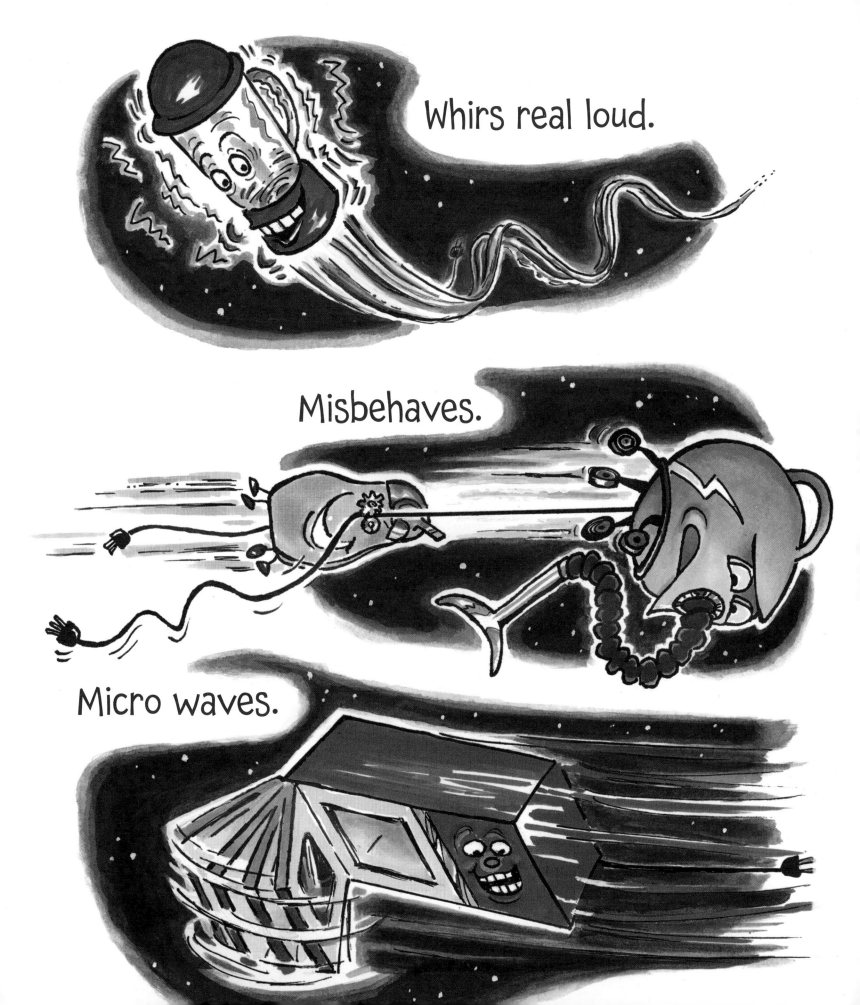

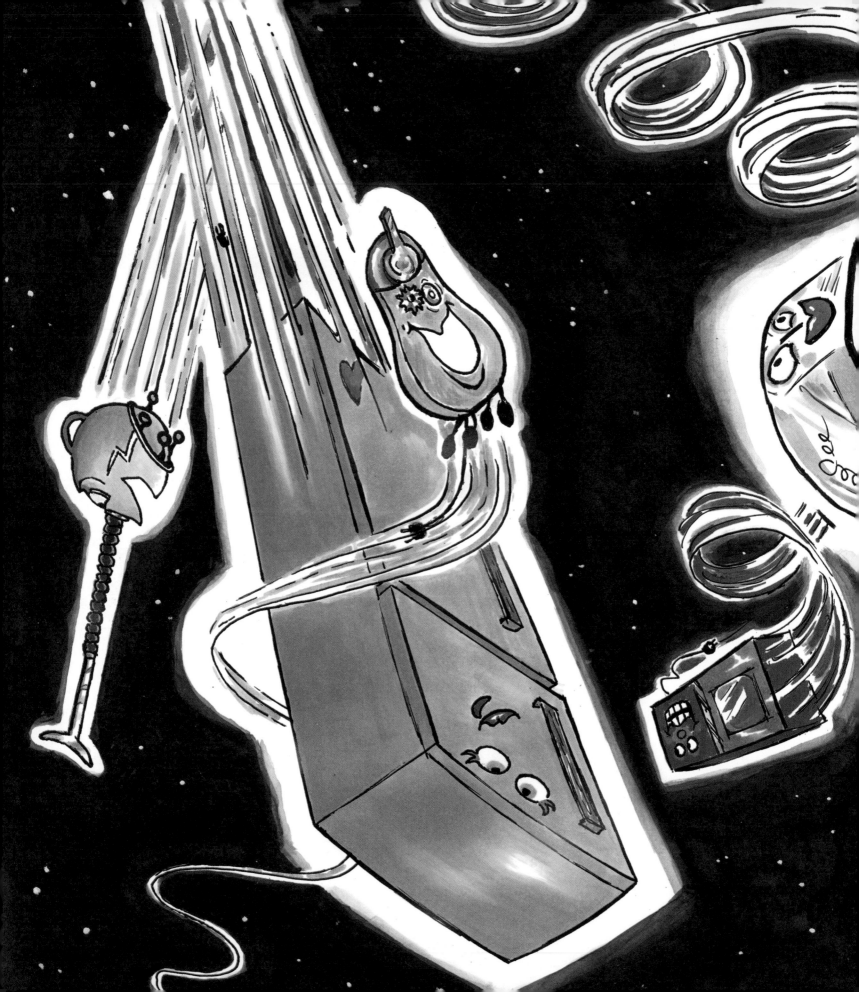

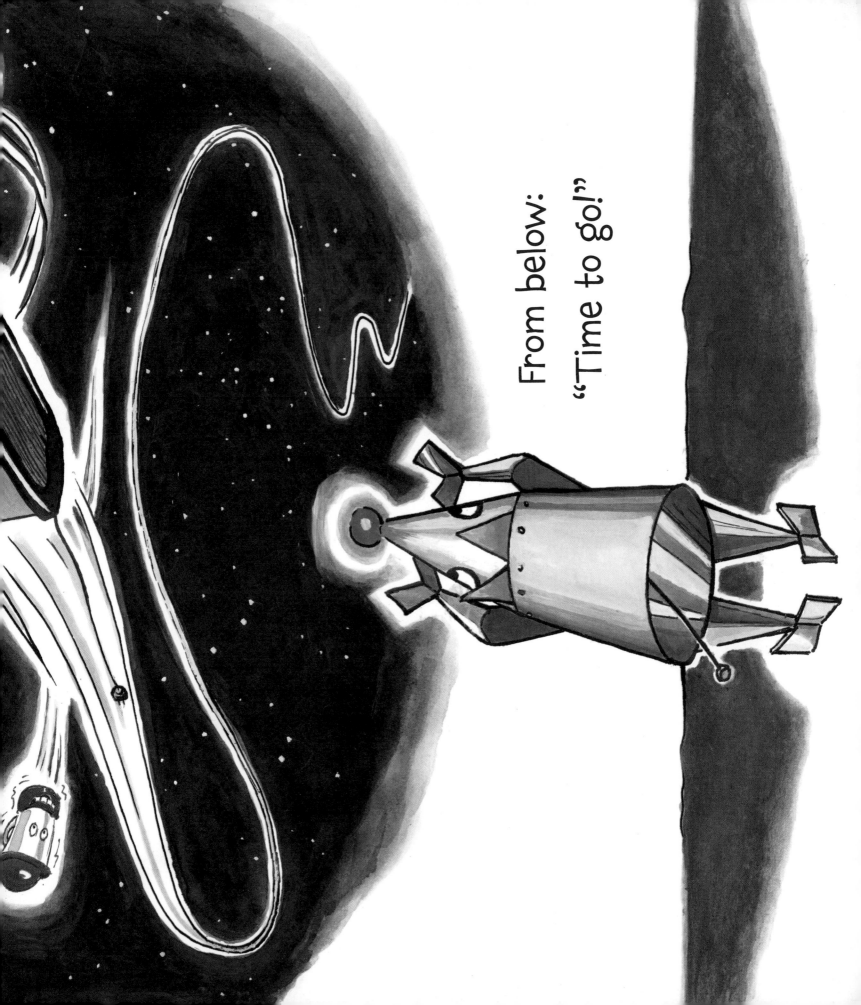

Gadgets glide back inside.

Up and down.

Still on ground.

Walks by pup.

Climbs on up.

Closes hatch.

"My ball glows."

"Fits my nose."

Starts to lift.
Special gift!

"Bow-wow-wow.
Beep-beep-pow!!!"

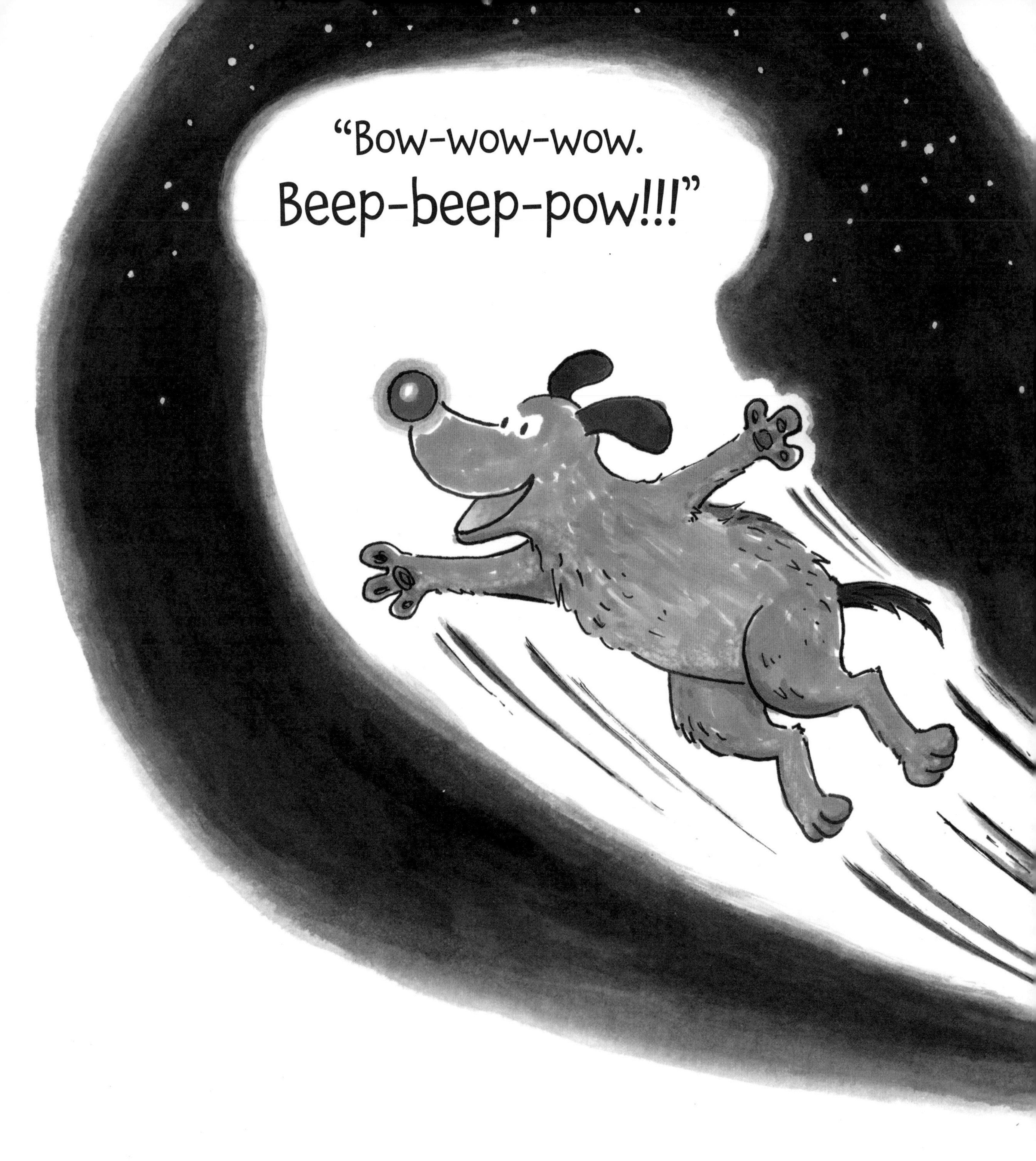

To the moon.

"Come back soon!"